Secret life of

A House Wife

Acknowledgments:

I just want to say thank you to my support system, my family, friends and my wonderful editor, I love you all so much. Thank you for believing in me.

-

"When you show gratitude, you're able to remember that you didn't arrive in this place in your journey by yourself. You had help, you had support, you had guidance."

-Angela Bassett

Secret Life of a House Wife Copyright © 2022

Amirah's Book Collection LLC

Amirah Suggs

All rights reserved. No part of this book may be reproduced in any form, or by any means without prior consent of the publisher, except brief quotes used in reviews.

This is a work of fiction. Any references or similarities to actual events, real events, living or dead, or to real locales are intended to give the novel a sense of reality. Any similarity in other names, characters, places, and incidents is entirely coincidental.

Editor: Bonner Revisions LLC

Dedication

This book is for every woman that loved a man so deeply that she forgot to love herself…

For the women that make mistakes unapologetically, and learn from them in silence.

And, the families that suffer in the end…

Simply because everyone must pay for the mistakes they've made.

1.

Lynne Walker seemed to have it all, including the looks. She had smooth caramel skin, long, bronzed legs that seemed endless, and stunningly flawless dark hair with hints of red that could only be seen whenever it was kissed by the sun. Her gorgeous tresses hung past the arch in her lower back and had a natural swing when she walked. She embodied beauty and brains, but also radiated a quiet, submissive power. At first glance, you would be afraid you'd crack her in half if you grabbed her too hard.

She had a beautiful daughter and a doting husband that loved her beyond words. They had a beautiful six-bedroom home, beach front in California. Her morning work-out consisted of a 6-mile run along the coast. As soon as she got back from her run, her husband would give her that animalistic gleam; the one that said I need you now. So right before he would leave for work every day, she would make love with her husband. It was a routine, and one she depended on faithfully. The romance and love making was on the top list of her priorities because keeping their marriage fresh and healthy was the only option. She loved her husband, and wanted the mutual feelings to remain. John gave Lynne feelings she never felt before, and it was something she had become obsessed with. She melted with his every touch to her body.

As she was finishing her workout, she couldn't help reliving her morning romp with her husband. With an anticipatory shiver and a smile, she replayed it in her mind.

"I love you," Lynne moaned as John inserted inside of her, causing her legs to tingle. He moved slowly and it felt like he had pressed into her soul. She knew that she would climax long before he did. He always made sure, and knew every inch to touch to make it happen.

After her first, he continued to stroke slowly. As the build-up came creeping up for her second, he choked out, "I love you too," and they both tumbled together on the bed.

Coming out of her memory, Lynne smiled as she ran in to her back yard and decided that another round was due that evening.

John was a businessman. At the age of fifty-two he had bought and sold over 500 properties across The United States, and had several property management companies that expanded from those business transactions. He provided a great life for Lynne, even though she was fully capable of taking care of herself, if necessary. He wanted her to have everything she ever wanted out of life, so the bills weren't something she ever had to worry about. To John, that was the personal priority that he worked towards, and he made it his job to do it well. A happy wife makes a happy life, he always told himself. This specific morning, he was getting packed to leave for Tennessee. There was a mansion there he wanted to remodel and sell, and had to go finalize the deal.

"Honey, how long will you be in Tennessee?" Lynne murmured groggily while still lying in bed. She was still thinking about the passionate morning workout.

"Not long baby, I should be back in three days," John called back from the shower.

Lynne got out of bed, preparing to get ready for her day as well. She was picking their daughter up from the airport that afternoon. She was so proud of Kenzie's accomplishments. Kenzie was only twenty-two years old, and she already knew exactly where she was going in life. She had time, but was excited that she was going to be home for the whole summer.

Looking in to the bathroom, she got another idea. "Well then," She replied silkily, "maybe one more for the road?" And jumped in the shower with him. After he had left for the airport, she made some coffee and went out to sit on her back veranda. Taking in the piercing blue of the ocean, and the light breeze that played around her, she lit her cigarette. Closing her eyes, she took a deep, cleansing breath. It was going to be a good day.

She heard her phone ring and went back in to grab it. Looking down, she smiled as her daughter's name came across the screen.

"Mom, remember, I'll be at the airport at 2 pm.," Kenzie said in the phone verifying her flight details.

"I'll be there don't worry. I can't wait to see you!" Lynne gushed.

After they hung up, Lynne finished her smoke and went to get dressed. On the way to the airport Lynne played her slow jams and reminisced about all the fun times with her daughter she always had.

When she approached the airport, Kenzie was waiting outside. Lynne's face lit up.

"Mommy, I missed you!" Kenzie exclaimed as she dropped her bags to the floor and ran towards her mom.

"My baby!" Lynne laughed as she embraced her daughter. "I missed you!"

The car ride seemed far too short as they laughed like they always do and caught up on all the gossip they hadn't talked about on the phone.

"So, is dad home?"

Lynne hesitated. "He will be back in a couple of days."

When they pulled up back at the house, Lynne went to make coffee while Kenzie went upstairs to unpack. She was so happy to have her daughter back for the summer. It was lonely at times with John being gone so much, so this was going to be fun. As the coffee was brewing, she heard Kenzie's phone ringing on the table. She noticed Arielle's name on the caller id, and yelled up to Kenzie. "Phone's ringing, its Arielle!"

Kenzie came jogging in to the kitchen and grabbed the phone. She always had a giddy look when it came to Arielle. "Hey girl!"

Arielle and Kenzie had been friends since they were little girls in elementary school. Arielle never really had any family. Her mom wasn't very supportive, nor did she do anything to raise Arielle the way a mother was supposed to. When she got older, she applied for housing through the state and she got approved. She currently lived in Tennessee with her daughter. Arielle and Kenzie were the exact same age, but she had her daughter when she was only fifteen. Lynne always thought Arielle was a bad influence on Kenzie and that they lead two completely different lives, but Kenzie loved her. Lynne grew to love Arielle and eventually began to treat her just like her own daughter. Whenever Arielle needed help, Lynne would wire her money to help with rent, food, or whatever Arielle may say she needed. She often tried to help as much as she could because she didn't want Kenzie sending her money while she was in college.

She looked over at her daughter laughing on the phone, and she smiled. She was happy she was home. "Everything ok with Arielle?" She asked when Kenzie hung up.

"Yes," She replied, a little hesitant.

"Are you sure? Anything you want to talk about?"

"No, everything is ok," She replied, grabbing her coffee quickly.

Lynne let it go. She knew her daughter, and knew she would eventually tell her when she was ready, so she let it go.

"So," she turned to Kenzie with a brilliant smile, "how about nails, hair and shopping tomorrow?"

"Love it!"

2.

Lynne and Kenzie spent the next two days spending some quality girl time; shopping, nails, hair, drinks and just general catching up. They were having so much fun, she almost forgot her husband was coming back home today and she needed to pick him up from the airport later that afternoon. Kenzie had left early that morning to go to the gym and meet up with some old friends. Lynne knew she had the morning to herself to relax and prepare for her husband's homecoming. He would be so excited to see Kenzie and they would all probably go out as a family later that night.

Lynne got up and made herself some fresh coffee and sat on the back veranda. With her coffee and a smoke, she called her long time best friend, Katherine. She and Katherine had been friends since they were in their twenty's and they never lost contact. Every morning they would have a gossip hour with their coffee. Katherine lives a little wild in Arizona, so during these sessions she would recap to Lynne all the crazy things that were going on with her. Her current craze was describing in detail all the men she was having affairs with now because she never got over her husband's affair two years prior.

"I do what I want now because he broke our vows a long time ago," Katherine continued when she was met with silence on the line. "All of that traveling he did, and I trusted that bastard. He left me alone, never invited me on any of the trips he had to take, and now we see why."

"Kat, I understand your pain, but if you don't want to be married any more than just leave him. You having an affair only makes it worse for you,"

Lynne replied after a long pause and a rub of her temple.

"Well, he pays for everything. I have no worries, and I'm content where I am. I wouldn't give that up for anybody, especially to another woman," Katherine responded with a laugh.

Katherine had been having multiple affairs for over a year since her husband broke her heart. She hasn't been right since.

I guess that's how some women get over it, Lynne thought.

"I wouldn't know what to do if John cheated on me. I would probably kill him," Lynne said to Katherine.

"Exactly. You haven't been in my shoes so you don't know how it feels to live it. Imagine giving a man your all; everything you had inside of you! You help him live out all his hopes and dreams, and then in one moment of weakness he destroys everything you are as a woman! Don't tell me anything about love! I'm going to get mine and still keep everything I worked hard to build, I promise you that!" Katherine shouted to Lynne, "and the guy who I have been seeing these past few weeks puts my body in a whole other world. Lynne, when he touches me, it feels like heaven on earth, and he's way better in bed than my husband." They both laughed.

"In all seriousness though, Lynne. I never thought this would happen to me. He treated me like gold, and then one day, it is someone else. Even the most loving faithful husband can destroy you. You must be careful, and always keep your guard up. It can happen to anyone; even the most faithful can fall."

Lynne loved her best friend. Katherine had been there with her from the beginning and they had been through hell and back together to get where they were in life. Lynne respected Katherine in every way and if she needed to cope and live her life the way she needed to, then so be it. But that last comment did give her a bad shiver.

"Where is my Kenzie at?" she continued, changing the subject. "I want to tell her that I love her and miss her."

"She's out with some friend's right now and I think she went to the gym earlier this morning, because she used my membership to get in," Lynne replied.

"Well you tell her that I love her and I can't wait to see her when I come out before the end of summer," Katherine said.

"I will, she will be so excited to see you too," Lynne agreed.

For a moment after they hung up, Lynne thought about her marriage and how much she loved John and rolled it around with that comment from Katherine. She really doesn't know if he has ever cheated while gone on one of those business trips, or if another woman has ever even been in the picture because of how much she trusted him. He never acted suspicious, and Lynne wasn't the type to look through phones or try to discover things. She just knew she loved him and he loved her. She knew he provided a wonderful life for her and her daughter. She has been happy ever since she can remember. At the same time, she realized how often she pushed her sadness to the side. With her mind wandering, she couldn't help her feelings.

I miss him so much. Him being gone on business trips all the time takes a toll on me. I have never thought about being with another man, but I do get lonely sometimes. John is the man of my dreams. I wouldn't have stayed married so long if I didn't truly love him. I know he has to work to continue to provide this lifestyle we are all used to, including Kenzie. Sometimes, I want him to just call in sick, stay home and kiss all over me, or talk about when we first met and eat food together in bed. It's just that sometimes I feel like a prop and that is it. When John is home he treats me to dinner, makes love to me, watches movies, and even rubs my feet at night. I just want that more often; I want that every night. I want my husband to be home with me. Is this lifestyle worth it? Is it worth living with this loneliness? I know he loves me and I know he would do anything for me, including working closer to home. That would just mean that a lot of what we have and the life we live would be so different. Can I give that up?

Dragging her mind back to the present, Lynne put out her cigarette and decided to put the unhealthy thought behind her. After all, he was coming home today. She went back in to get ready to go pick John up from the airport. It had been too long since they had all been together as a family.

3.

Kenzie ran in the house and up to John's office and hugged him. "I missed you dad!"

"I missed you too baby girl," he said warmly, "I am so glad you are home."

"Me too! I feel like it has been forever! How are you? How are your properties going? How are you and mom?" Kenzie peppered him with questions as she perched on his desk.

"Slow down baby," John laughed. "You're going to be here all summer, take it easy."

Kenzie laughed remembering how funny her dad can be, and how much she missed him. They had been very close all her life.

"Oh, okay...well, Dad, I wanted to talk to you about something before I talk to mom," she said suddenly.

"Anything for you, princess," John joked as he playfully tugged on her hair.

"Well you know Arielle is dealing with a lot. Right now, apparently, she is mixed up with some man, and the way she talks it seems like it's getting serious, but not in a good way. Seeing that I haven't spent much time with her in a long time, and I'll be here all summer," she said snuggling up to him. "I wanted to know if we could pay for her to come visit and stay with us for a few weeks? I'm thinking the time away and out here with me will help her get back on the right track," Kenzie continued sweetly.

John hesitated. "You know that girl is like family, but honestly she is an adult now with a child. We can't rescue her from everything. It was different when she was a child herself, but as an adult, she needs to act like one and figure these things out herself. We love you and haven't seen you in a long time, and wanted this summer to be about family."

"You are right. I will make time to go out and see her at another time," Kenzie replied.

Kenzie bounded out of the office, and went to get ready for the family dinner.

Once at dinner, Lynne looked around at her family and chided herself for ever having doubts about her husband. As she smiled at him across the table, and looked left to her daughter, she was so grateful at the closeness of the two people that she loved the most. She sat back, pushed those thoughts away, and decided to be happy for what she had.

We haven't had a nice family dinner like that in a long time, Lynne thought as she jumped into the shower later that night. Allowing the water to caress her body, her mind wandered back to the conversation she had with Katherine earlier. She didn't want to say it to Katherine, but there were times when she had her suspicions and felt John was being dishonest. Then again, maybe it was just her own mind playing tricks on her. Usually when she was missing him those thoughts creeped in. *I have to stop thinking those thoughts. He is here now,* she thought, as her body started to tingle as the thought of what she wanted flashed in her mind.

"Babe, do you want to get in with me?" she shouted over the sound of the shower.

"No babe, I already took one, come to bed!" John shouted back.

Lynne could see him slightly through the fog in the mirror. He was on his laptop and seemed very distracted. *I can change that,* she thought with a wicked grin. She oiled her body up from head to toe and slipped into a slick black night gown.

Lynne lived for Johns' compliments; it was one of the reasons she always talked herself down when she started getting those suspicious feelings. She always, even after all their years together, made sure she looked her best for him, which is why when he didn't notice her or even look up for that matter, it put her back up. She slid in the bed next to him, and all she heard was a grunt.

"There's something I want to talk to you about," John said slowly, shutting his laptop.

"Kenzie came to me today about Arielle. She wanted to talk to me first, so please don't repeat it, Lynne. Anyway, she wanted Arielle to come here with us for a while."

"Oh, that would be…"

"I said no," he said forcefully, interrupting her. "This summer is about Kenzie being here and spending time as a family. We can't keep helping Arielle when she's in a rough patch. She will figure it out, or learn too." John continued, placing his hand on Lynne's thigh.

"Well babe, I don't understand why that would be a problem. Arielle is practically our second daughter," Lynne replied with a confused look on her face.

John grabbed Lynne by her throat and held her face to his, a repetitive motion that deemed the subject matter closed.

"I said no, Lynne." He kissed her forehead, with his grip still tight around her neck. The loving feeling was slipping and being replaced by fear in that moment. While all she could feel was the pain from his hands on her neck, she still felt a hint of pleasure from John's touch. His grip lightened, and turned in to a caress. Her mind and heart were at war.

The pain slipped into pleasure as he started to softly kiss and rub. John started moving his lips lower and lower until he reached Lynne's wetness. He took his fingers and ran them across her breasts. He kept his tongue inside of her and then started to move in and out just how she liked it. Lynne grabbed his head and pulled him up so she could return the pleasure. Lynne started by wrapping her lips around him, letting him set his own pace, and instructed him to move her head however he wanted to. John got lost inside of her mouth, and before he was finished he caressed her chin and kissed her on the forehead. As he led her back down to his manliness, he just held her there, and before she knew it, John exploded in that same position. As he was shuttering from the aftershock, she smiled, she couldn't help herself. This man was her everything. She looked up and whispered, "I love you."

4.

The next morning, Lynne woke up to a bouquet of Orchids on the bedside table. It was always the same after he was a little rough with her. John, of course, put them there with a note, usually with an apology. He was always smart, and never said what happened. All it usually said was, *please forgive me, I was wrong and I love you.* Which was why, picking up the note, Lynne felt nauseous. There was no apology. It was like he didn't realize what he had done; or worse, didn't care.

[12pm is lunch with Kenzie, I love you see you then. I had an early golf game with some potential investors. –John]

Lynne always admired his thoughtfulness. She looked around the bedroom, noting that it was already 10:30 am. Still holding her neck slightly, she just sat and imagined life without him. Even having a degree in law, she wouldn't know where to begin. John was the safely net. *He must not have realized how tight he had me.* Lynne's thoughts turned into excuses.

Deciding not to wallow in what it may or may not mean, or the weird reaction John had to the idea of Arielle coming out for the summer, she decided to indulge in a long hot bath, taking her time to get presentable. This time, there was a little red mark from where his fingers had pressed. *That is new*, she thought. Once in the bathroom, she decided she still looked tired so a facial while she decompressed was in order.

While relaxing in the tub, she heard her daughter shouting through her bedroom door.

"Mom are you almost ready? I'll drive."

She hadn't realized how long she had been soaking.

"20 minutes," Lynne shouted back as she stood up from the bathtub. She dried off quickly, pulled on the summer dress she had laid out the night before, and quickly and thoroughly applied her makeup, carefully covering the mark on her neck. The last thing she wanted was Kenzie to see it.

As she was finishing her hair, her thoughts kept roaming back to the conversation with her husband last night. I wanted to talk to Kenzie about Arielle, but I knew John would get angry with me, as he considered the matter closed. John had a mean streak at times, but I tried not to let it phase me and always tried to understand the type of pressure he was under. There was no reason to ever speak on it, so I don't.

Arielle and Kenzie had been friends since they were kids. We basically raised her. I know Arielle wasn't the best influence on her, but Kenzie loved her, and we grew to love her as well. The girl had been through hell. The girl had been taken advantage of at such a young age by everyone, including her own mother. She used to tell me that when she was younger her mother actually sold her to pay rent, or get her hands-on drugs. Whatever her mother needed, she used Arielle to get it. She literally gave that poor child to men to sleep with! She cried all the time, and never wanted to leave the house. It took a long time to get her to even be comfortable to sleep at our house. She was always terrified. By the age of 14 we found out she was on coke, and had moved in with an older man she barely knew. We found out two years later that he was whoring her out as well. By this time, she had gotten knocked up, and still has no clue who the father was. She had been raped, and beaten. The only stability that girl always had was us. *Why is John so against this?*

Her thoughts were interrupted by another shout from downstairs.

"Mom! We are going to be late!"

"I'll be right down!"

Grabbing her purse, she shook off the uneasy feeling she had and put on a brave smile for her daughter as she mentally prepared herself for lunch.

We arrived at Niche's café. This was Kenzie's favorite place to eat. John always made reservations here. I didn't even have to ask where we were going; I knew my husband. It still bothered me that he didn't want to drive together as a family. John was always on the move, and it hurt that it seemed like we were always second priority. Sometimes it felt like his business was his only priority.

During lunch, Kenzie told us all about everything she had going on in New York. I hated she was so far away, but if she was happy, it made me happy too. As I sat there with my family, I just thought about myself. All my dreams, all my goals; *where did the time go? How could I have not done one thing I wanted to do*? Smiling and laughing while Kenzie talked, she half listened. *My parents always wanted me to marry rich. They had this planned for me since I was a little girl; Pageants and modeling were the biggest part of my childhood. It seemed like I was never actually able to be a kid.* Looking across the table, she realized she couldn't go back, but that didn't mean she couldn't wish it sometimes. Her whole adulthood had been devoted to John and raising Kenzie. *Even the way we raised her had to be his way,* she thought. Everything was always his way. I loved this man, but sometimes I wondered just how much I loved myself.

In between the laughs and the conversations, I couldn't help but notice that during lunch, John stayed in his phone. I don't even remember him being fully engaged in much of the conversation.

Just smiles and agreements, couple of laughs is all that we seemed to get out of him. Kenzie loves her dad and hasn't seen him in a while, so I know she hasn't noticed the change.

As we were finishing up our lunch, I started becoming obsessive. *What was so damn important in that phone?* As we were going to leave, I kissed John, and right before I could say anything, he decided to drop the fact that he had to, once again, go out of town. *You just got back,* I thought with a fake smile frozen on my face. Instead, all I said was, "Really? So soon? Where do you have to go, and how long will you be gone?" As I said all of this, I saw his face. It had turned to stone. I asked too many questions.

I quickly changed gears so Kenzie wouldn't think anything was wrong. "Too many questions for lunch," I laughed lightly. "Just let me know when you need me to take you to the airport."

John's face changed from stone to charm so fast I almost lost my balance.

"I will let you know all the details later babe, I have another meeting tonight. I need to assess the work that still needs to be done, so I will know after that. I love both of you."

He kissed Kenzie and gave me another kiss and strolled quickly to his car.

As we drove home, my suspicions grew. That damn Katherine. I hated to admit it, but John was starting to show all the signs that Katherine explained about with the situation with her husband. I didn't let her know, but I started to question my marriage more after that last conversation. John had been going in and out of town since Kenzie had gotten here. *Wasn't he the one that said this summer was about her and spending quality time as a family?* With all the important meetings and business trips he seemed to have every day, I felt like I was seeing him less and less. Even between business trips, we were barely having sex anymore. My body was craving him, and my mind was becoming curious. 20 years of marriage, I think I deserved some time to be loved and appreciated. I have been a loving, loyal, subservient wife for the entirety of our marriage.

5.

Two days. John was home for two more days before he left, and was extremely distant the whole time. I, for the first time felt the urge to see what he has been up to. I never questioned him, but the way he had been acting towards me lately, I couldn't help it. Never out loud, though. Out loud questions tend to lead to accidents. John was in the shower, so I took a chance to see if I could get into his phone. I waited to see if he was going to play his music. John always put smooth jazz on when he needed some downtime. It was his go-to when he needed to fully relax and get his mind off work for a moment. It also meant it was going to be a long one. As I heard the sound of the saxophone spill into the air, I went for it. I had time.

I grabbed his phone, noticing there was a password on it. *That's weird.* John has never had a password on his phone before. As I set the phone back exactly as it was when I picked it up, I felt it vibrate. My heart pounded as I looked at the screen. A Stacey came up on his phone. I pressed on the name, and saw she said [call me].

I heard the water turn off and I hurried and placed the phone down. *That bastard.* My mind began to race. I knew I had to compose myself. *Don't let him see you know anything.* I knew something had to be going on. That disloyal piece of shit! I started to remember what my mom told me a long time ago; never tell a man all that you know. Play your part. A man will always be a man.

I quickly jumped into bed and pulled the covers over my head. I closed my eyes and prayed for sleep.

During yoga the next morning, I thought about John and our marriage. I wasn't important to him, I didn't matter. The man I loved didn't love me. *Did he love her? Was their sex life better than ours?* I gave that man my youth. As I replayed my mother's words again, it made me realize that maybe my dad wasn't any better. Why else would she give me advice like that? Then I remembered what Katherine had gone through, and what she had told me. 'Even the most faithful can fall.' *How could I have been so stupid, and so blind?* She cursed herself under her breath. To believe my husband was different, what would make me that special? I knew John better than he knew himself. I was naive. All those different smells coming from his clothes, the lack of eye contact when we spoke, the new sex positions he offered to me, the rare times he does anymore, I should have known it was another woman.

"Breathe," the yoga instructor said softly as she raised her hands to the top of the mat.

I couldn't breathe, I couldn't think. I felt the short quick breaths. The anxiety was coming. I had the perfect life. Well, what I thought was a perfect life. You can do everything for a man, give him every piece of your being, and he still will screw you.

What do I do? Do I tell him? Do I tell my daughter? Do I leave and just never speak to him again? I was losing my shit. I had no idea how I was going to handle this. I had to stop thinking about it right now. Yoga was supposed to be helping me. I focused on my breathing the rest of the session.

After yoga, I just sat in my car. John called me as he surprisingly still did every day to see how my day was going. I debated on if I should pick it up. It kept ringing. With a deep breath and shaky hands, I answered.

"Hey baby, I've been calling you, is everything ok?" John asked sincerely.

"Hi baby, yes everything is fine. Yoga ran over and I chatted with the ladies after," I replied with tears stinging my eyes.

"Well, I just wanted to check in and make sure everything was ok. I love you," John said, his voice rushed.

"Love yo- ", she was cut off at the sound of a click. He hung up. She stared dumfounded at her phone. How dare he hang up!

It all made sense though. Of course he was in a hurry to hang up. The liar! The cheater!

I screamed, smacking the steering wheel.

As the day went by, all Lynne did was cry. Whenever she heard Kenzie coming, she would dry her face or reapply her makeup quickly trying to hide it, but Kenzie could tell something was going on. Whenever she asked, Lynne ensured her that everything was okay.

With John still out of town, Lynne had a lot of time to think. As the days went by, the tears turned to rage, and all her thoughts became about revenge.

How dare he do this. The pain in her heart made her start to wonder what that woman had over her. Who could have made John risk it all? Lynne had to know. Since John was back in Tennessee and Lynne was very familiar with his work there, as that was his most repeated traveling location, she felt like it was time to pay him a visit. She pulled out her phone and decided to get her plans together.

6.

I just had to see it for myself; I had to know, I had to be sure. Could Stacey have been a coworker, or business partner? Why would she text him at 11pm? I kept trying to make excuses, make it innocent in my head because I loved him, but I knew better. John wouldn't ask questions if I said I was taking a trip. He was always so busy at this time of the year, and his mind would be elsewhere. Just to seal the deal I called John ahead of time.

"Babe, hey. I've been missing Katherine lately. I'm thinking about taking a trip out to see her, spend a couple of days catching up."

"Hey babe, I think that is a great idea. You two always have so much fun together, and I think you could use that time with her. I know I have been gone a lot this summer. You deserve a trip too."

Her stomach did a nervous summer sault. "I will let you know the flight details as soon as I have them set."

"I have to go baby, but yes just let me know."

"I will."

Silence. He hung up again! This time, without an I love you. The sadness and anger were battling in her mind and stomach.

She dropped her phone in her purse with vengeance in her eyes. Leaving a note for Kenzie that she would be back in a few days, she grabbed only an overnight bag and headed to the airport. On her way, she booked one flight. When she walked in to the airport, she booked another one.

I knew John would be at one of two hotels. In the morning, I decided just to call them both and see what I could figure out. With my stomach filled with knots, I dialed the first. When the front desk answered, all I said was, "Mr. John Walker's room please," and waited for the response.

"I am sorry, he isn't currently checked in here, were you sure it was Walker?"

"I am so sorry, yes. I must have dialed the wrong one. This is where he stayed last visit, silly me. Thank you for your time." My heart was racing as I hung up. Now I knew exactly where he was. I decided I wasn't going to call, but just show up. I didn't want anyone telling him I called. It was a good thing he wasn't at the other hotel.

I gathered my wits and walked up to the reception desk.

"Hi, is John Walker checked in here? I am his wife and was hoping to surprise him," I told the cheery hotel clerk sweetly, batting my eyes. After answering questions that could verify I was his wife, the front desk clerk hesitantly confirmed. "You have been so helpful, thank you!" As I turned away, the happy smile hardened, and my eyes turned cold.

I waited back in my car. I wanted to be secretive about this, but I didn't know how I would do it.

Then it hit me. I went back inside and told the hotel clerk exactly what was going on. She was a young girl with really nothing to lose. I told her I had reasons to believe he was cheating on me, and I just needed to know for myself. *I should have been an actress,* I thought as I played the desperate, devastated housewife. I was, but at this point I was at the pissed off stage. She seemed very intrigued with the story, and had a look like she knew something, but I didn't catch her hesitation. This was a very upscale hotel, and scandal wasn't exactly publicized here. I told her all I wanted to do was catch him and I swore I wouldn't make a scene.

I let her know she wouldn't even know I was there, and neither would John.

Lynne didn't want to confront him, just wanted proof. Pressed for time because he was out from the hotel now, I secured the deal by giving her $600 dollars. I had money to spend, and this was the perfect investment. The clerk took the money, but not before telling me to put it in the bathroom in the first stall. She was a smart girl; she knew there were cameras in the lobby and had no intention on letting this come back on her. My tears, although scripted, were internally real. Pissed off stage or not, I was still hurting. She caved though, and she made me a key to his room. when she handed me a key card, my body felt like it was going to go into shock. I couldn't believe I was here and about to catch the man I have loved for all these years having an affair. God, please let me be wrong.

Lynne took the elevator up to his room and knocked first. She had to be sure no one was in there. When no one answered, she looked both ways down the hall and slipped the key in the door. When she saw the green light that she had access, she felt physically sick. The emotional roller coaster she had been on was exhausting. She opened the door and slipped in. She started looking around. The smell of sex and perfume filled the room. She could smell his favorite cologne. The Yeon by men was all over the place. The panic subsided again, and was replaced again with rage. Her beautiful green eyes hardened as she continued to look around. To Lynne's surprise, there were no woman's belongings in the room. *Should that make me feel better, or worse?* The fear of John walking in at any moment put a bad feeling in the air. He could really have a temper sometimes. A quick memory flashed into her mind.

It was late at night and we had just returned home from a dinner with some of John's potential clients.

He was upset that the deal wasn't going to go through as he planned. I must have pissed him off at some point because all I said was 'babe maybe it just wasn't the right time,' and John slapped me right across the face. I fell to the floor but not before hitting my head on the edge of the bed frame. I couldn't even remember him saying sorry, but only bringing in Orchids and gifts that made me always forget when he became abusive.

I snapped out of my memories and decided to hide in the closet. He had to come back sometime. John had a suite on the top floor at the hotel. The hotel room was huge; a living room that was as big as our bedroom, four closets, a huge king size bed, a full kitchen with a balcony designed to dine. This luxurious suite was surprising to me, being that he was on a business trip. He always said that the boring hotel rooms were nothing compared to home. For a hotel, this was pretty comparable to me. I turned my phone on silent to be sure I didn't get any incoming calls. Right as I was switching it over, Katherine called. I knew I had to answer. I had forgot to check in with her. Seeing she was my alibi, I had to talk to her. My mind had been going a hundred miles per hour.

"Hi Kat," Lynne whispered.

"Lynne where have you been all day, and why are you whispering? Girl, we talk every day. What's going on?" Katherine demanded in her sassy voice.

"Katherine, I can't talk right now, but if John calls you, or Kenzie, make sure you say I am sleeping, or out for a run, or anything, but make sure they think we are together," Lynne said quickly.

"Lynne, what the hell…"

"Kat, please, I'll call you in a couple of hours and explain everything. Please just trust me, love you. I have to go."

The moment I hung up, I heard the door open. Holy shit it was John. I hurried and turned my phone off and stayed completely still in the closet, with my door slightly cracked. I watched as John walked in. He was wearing his all dark blue suit, perfectly tailored with the tie I purchased him for Christmas. I loved him in a tie. John had the most beautiful body. His bald head and his beautiful skin always made me weak in the knees. John was a perfectionist, with charm to kill. Why do you think I was hiding in the closet?

I continued to watch as John started to take off his suit jacket and undo his tie. He undid the top two buttons on his shirt and his chest hair slightly peaked out. He sat down by his bed on the chair. And covered his face with his hands for a moment. He looked up, and looked directly at the closet I was in. My heart was pounding so loud I thought maybe he heard it. He got back up and went into the drawer of the bedside table and pulled out a cigar. I watched as he opened the balcony door so the smoke would billow out, and clear the air as he smoked. His phone rang and he answered on the first ring.

"Come up, I'm here," John said to the voice on the other end of the phone. My stomach caved in and I felt chills run up my arms. I pressed back into the closet, knowing this would be the end to my denial, and give me the truth that I so desperately needed. I just knew I would have to live with this and decide how I want my life to be. John knew I loved him more than anything in the world. He knew he was the only man I truly loved, and yet, he could do this to me. I heard John head to the door and as he opened the door, a woman's voice caressed the air.

"Baby, I missed you. Don't you keep me waiting that long again," the woman's voice purred through the closet and sent icicles down my spine. As I took a second to process this, I couldn't help but notice that voice was familiar, almost like I've heard it a million times. I was sure that I made no noises, but I held my breath and moved closer to the inch of a crack that I could see out of. I hesitated, then looked. I waited until John moved out of sight so I could see the woman. The moment he stepped aside, I felt all the life drain from my body. I wanted to kill them both. I took shallow breaths, and tried not to pass out after the biggest shock of my life.

Gripping the sides of the closet to contain her balance, she looked on to see what was going to happen.

She heard a giggle, and then watched as that little slut undressed John. He pulled her closer, and pulled her dress over her head.

I looked over as I saw John's manhood standing tall. So did she. She grabbed it and stroked it up and down, as I watched and listened to him begging her to let him inside of her.

The tears were hard and fast, but I swiped the back of my hand over my face, and forced myself to keep watching. This was the proof I needed. I had to finish it out. As I felt my heart shatter, I focused on my husband, and the fact that I was betrayed by two of the last people I ever thought would hurt me.

As I looked on, I saw her bend down and take him in her mouth. He moaned, and it was a sound I had never heard before. As I saw him finish, he pulled her up, so gently, and lifted her up and wrapped her naked body around his waist. He walked her to the bed as they fed off each other. The way they were going at it, you would think they were starved for each other. He laid her on the bed and spread her legs open. As his head went down, I felt my food come up. *Oh my God I am going to be sick.*

Covering her mouth, she forced herself to watch it through to the end.

He was still going down on her, running his tongue over her thighs, and back in her. He focused for so long Lynne couldn't help but think how he never spent that much focus on her pleasure. His head came up. He looked down at her, spread out, eyeing him like candy. He smiled, took a shot of what looked like tequila, and crooked his finger at her. She crawled seductively to him, and he lifted her up again. She wrapped her legs back around him as he spun to position himself on the bed. He slowly lowered her on to his shaft, and started moaning.

I watched as she grinded up and down on him, with her head thrown back and him feasting on her breasts. Then he flipped her over, and I punished myself as I watched him take her from behind and rub and kiss on her ass. I couldn't watch it anymore. I sat curled in a ball in the corner of the closet and covered my ears and focused on my breathing. If I didn't, someone was going to die. It was a mixture of rage, humiliation and pain. At the moment, I couldn't tell which emotion was winning. Suddenly they got louder, and I knew it was almost over. All I heard was him climaxing and shouting her name.

"Awe shit, Arielle," John's breath hitched as he finished pouring himself into her.

Lynne had to get out of there, but she was paralyzed in place.

7.

What was I thinking? Why would I put myself in this position? Now I'm stuck here until they leave, Lynne thought in a panic. She had to get out of there. She couldn't watch another round. She thought back to her breathing practices and put her head down between her legs and focused. Her brain racing, her rage focused on Arielle.

How could she? Arielle was like a daughter to me. I helped her when her mother didn't. I took her into my home, I allowed her to be a bad influence on my daughter and still saw the good in her. The nerve!

This is who he had been going out of town to see? She is the reason why I never see my husband anymore? All those late-night phone calls and early flights; it all made sense. How long had this been going on? Lynne felt nauseous again, praying that this hadn't been going on since she was a child. Somehow in between all the thoughts and questions, I fell asleep.

I woke up in the morning groggy and in pain having slept in the closet.

Peeking out of the closet, she waited a beat to see if she could figure out what time it was. She wanted to wait until John checked out before coming out. Her next fear was him catching her in town. I watched them walk back in to the bedroom, and caught the ending of their conversation.

Arielle looked annoyed, and John looked like he was trying to leave. "I have to get back home, I'll be back to you soon," John said to Arielle, as he kissed her long and hard.

"Are you really going to do it this time?" Arielle asked with a hint of frustration and a hand on her hip.

"I am going to leave her. I promise," John replied.

When I heard those words, my knees weakened. I couldn't fully grasp how I ended up here. He really was in love with her; a kid, someone who grew up with our daughter. Someone who could be his daughter. This was the ultimate disrespect. Arielle left, and John was gathering his things. It looked like he was getting ready to check out. As he left, I cut my phone back on to see what time it was. When it came up, I saw it was past 11:00 am. John was finally checking out. I knew as soon as he was gone I would be able to sneak out of here. She burst out of the closet door and threw open the balcony doors. She needed air. She stood there for a moment and took a few deep breaths. She called a cab and headed down to the lobby. When her cab pulled up, she got in and finally her chest didn't feel so constricted. She had been feeling claustrophobic ever since she landed in Tennessee. The first thing she thought to do was call Kenzie.

I can't let my daughter know what is going on just yet, I thought to myself. I honestly didn't know how I was going to tell her. Kenzie would be crushed.

"Hey Kenzie," I said into the phone.

"Mom, where have you been I called you last night. I called auntie Katherine, she said you went to sleep early. You must have had a great time," Kenzie said with a laugh.

"Yes, we had a great time. I fell asleep early. It has been a long time since I went out like that, I couldn't hang." She laughed, hoping it sounded sincere. "My phone went dead, I am so sorry I didn't call you when I got in. I must have needed the rest," She said to reassure her, and feeling guilty lying to her.

"I'll be back tomorrow I think. We are going to just hang out here and recover. It has been just like old times."

"Well have fun mom, seriously. You deserve it. I love you!"

"Love you too, and I will call you a little later today with my flight plans."

After we hung up, I saw that John texted me twice last night. He didn't even call. In between his wonderful night, he managed to text me saying, hey babe, I love you, be home in a few days. Then another message read: Have a good night baby. That asshole, I mumbled to myself.

I couldn't cry anymore. It was no longer just about me. Now he was hurting Kenzie. His daughter. Did he really think this wouldn't destroy her? I didn't know how to save her from this pain. Not only the loss of her closest friend, but learning of the betrayal of her father, and realizing that he was a man with no morals or values. Something had to be done. He had to be taught a lesson. I had to put my plan into motion.

Lynne called Katherine right away.

"Katherine I'm coming over, I should be there by 4:00 pm. I'm trying to book this 1:00 pm flight," I said while in process of paying online.

"Lynne, I had to think fast when Kenzie called. You never called me back what the hell is going on?"

"Katherine, I am coming to your house. I need to speak to you privately. I will explain it all. It's John, Katherine. He's been cheating.

"Lynne, what? When? With Who? For How long?" She kept firing questions at her.

"I will see you soon," I replied, exhausted.

I made it to the airport. I still haven't heard from John since last night. I sent him a text just to see if I would get a response.

[Hey babe, staying over at Katherine's for another day. See you tomorrow.]

I got to the airport and still no call. I got on my flight and slept like the dead the whole flight.

When I landed, I picked up a rental car and headed to Katherine's.

Katherine was waiting on the porch when Lynne pulled up.

"My husband is at the gym. What the hell is going on?" Katherine demanded as soon as Lynne got out of the car. Lynne dropped onto the porch and began to tell her friend everything that had happened in this past week. She told her how she flew to Tennessee and how she managed to gain access to John's hotel room. She told her everything she saw. Katherine couldn't believe he was sleeping with Arielle.

"I told you there was something about that little girl I never liked!" Katherine shouted.

Lynne watched as Katherine paced back and forth, vibrating anger. She couldn't hold in her emotions anymore. "How could he do this to you Lynne! That piece of shit!" Katherine went on and on. "You have to tell Kenzie. Leave his ass Lynne."

Katherine's voice kept rising. "You have always been a better woman than me. I know I didn't leave my husband when he cheated on me, but you gave up everything for that man. You treated him like gold. You, of all people do not deserve this."

Katherine knew how Lynne was feeling. She felt this same pain with her own husband. But Katherine knew she was stronger than Lynne, and not nearly as innocent as Lynne was. Being her friend for over 30 years, she knew her. She knew how this would affect her. She knew her nights would be long and her days would be filled with regret, and it would destroy her over time. Lynne wasn't a cheater. She devoted her entire world to John as if he was a higher power. Katherine never liked the idea of Lynne being overly in love with him, but she was her friend, and they were always there for each other so she always supported her.

"I can't even gather myself to tell Kenzie, Katherine. I haven't even let on to John that I know anything. Oh, Katherine you should have seen them," Lynne said with tears filling her eyes.

The way she looked, Katherine couldn't tell anymore if they were sad tears or angry tears.

They got up and went to the back deck. Katherine grabbed a bottle of wine and placed it in front of Lynne as she lit up a cigarette. Lynne filled her lungs with puff after puff. Katherine hit her own cigarette and watched her friend, and waited. "He has hit me before Kat," Lynne blurted out quietly in between puffs.

"He what, Lynne? How could you keep that from me?" Katherine jumped up out of her seat.

"It doesn't happen often. I can literally count on one hand how many times, but I just wanted to tell you.

You're my best friend, and finally I can get that out. John gets so angry at times," Lynne went on.

Fury began to fill the air. Katherine's skin felt like boiling water as she looked at her friend.

"So Lynne, what are you going to do?" Katherine asked the question as she poured her friend another glass of red wine.

Right as Lynne was about to answer, her phone rings.

"Don't you dare answer that phone," Katherine demanded.

"I have to. This has to be on my time." Lynne's voice hardened.

"Hey babe. How's it going?" John asked as soon as Lynne answered.

"Hi. I am still at Katherine's house," Lynne said trying to sound as normal as possible. Katherine was giving her a look to remind her to remain calm and to not let on that there's a problem.

"Oh that's good. Tell Katherine I said hello. Listen, babe. I have to stay a little longer to deal with some things with the property here in Tennessee. I should be home in another week or so. When I come home,

I want to spend some time with you. Just me and you."

"That sounds nice, but what about Kenzie, John? You should spend some time with her. She's only here for a few more weeks," Lynne said feeling annoyed.

"Lynne, I got my daughter, ok? You don't worry about that. I have to provide, don't I? I will see you both soon. Love you. I have to go," John hung up.

Katherine jumped up from her seat with her cigarette still in hand and waited for her to talk.

"He wants to spend time with me. He told Arielle that he was leaving me, Kat. That's the only part I didn't tell you. That is why he wants to spend time with me." Lynne put her head back and rubbed her temple.

"Lynne, get on your phone and book us a flight. We're going to Tennessee."

Lynne looked at her closest friend and saw the same rage that she felt radiating off her. Without response, she picked her phone back up and booked the flights. They were leaving in two hours.

8.

We didn't speak the whole flight. Katherine looked like she was ready to commit murder, and I was exhausted. When we landed, we grabbed a rental car and Katherine drove us to the hotel I had told her he was at. The hotel clerk said John Walker had already checked out.

We walked back outside, and in my heart, I knew where he was.

"What if he is at Arielle's house?" Katherine asked, speaking out loud what Lynne was thinking.

I know he is, Lynne thought. She knew where Arielle lived. Of course she did. She had been sending that girl money and gifts and ordering groceries from across the country to be delivered for years now. Her house was paid for through the state. *At least we didn't pay for that.* Without a second thought, Lynne drove to her house. The whole way there, all Lynne focused on was the pain she felt, the anger and the sadness, and bitterness filled her face. All she wanted was to break him how he broke her. That's all he deserved. Arielle's house was a half hour away from the hotel. They creeped slowly to a stop about four houses down.

Katherine couldn't believe her eyes. John was standing outside, kissing Arielle. She looked over at Lynne, saw the anger, the sadness, and physically felt the pain for her friend. After the public display of affection ended, which seemed like hours even though it was only minutes, they watched Arielle get into her car. John must have purchased it for her because there was no way Arielle could afford a 2023 Jeep Wrangler. John walked back in to her house as Arielle pulled off.

"That son of a bitch!" Katherine shouted smacking the dashboard.

"I told you he was seeing her, Kat. I just can't believe this was happening right under my nose, and Kenzie's nose as well," Lynne replied while lighting a cigarette from her pack. She never smoked this much, but her nerves were bad, and there was nothing else she could do to bring them down.

"You need to confront him. Here. Now," Katherine said vehemently.

"Katherine, I can't, I just can't," Lynne said, torn between emotions.

In that moment, Katherine knew she had to be there for her friend. Lynne had always been there for her. Even in the worse days, Lynne was someone she could always count on.

"Fine, I will," Katherine said matter-of-factly.

"No Kat, don't!" Lynne hissed as she tried to pull Katherine back as she opened the door.

Lynne couldn't grab her in time. She watched as Katherine walked up to the door and knocked.

"Katherine, what the hell are you doing here?!" John exclaimed, shocked as he looked around before grabbing her by the arm and pulling her inside.

Lynne couldn't let Katherine be in there alone. She knew this was her battle and she needed to finally stand up to him. Lynne never thought she would be in this situation but there was no turning back.

She threw the door open and walked into the house. There was Katherine screaming at John as he sat on the couch and puffed his cigar as if he could care less what she was shouting about.

"Oh, there she is," John replied with a sneer on his face as he took another puff.

Lynne didn't know how she remained so calm. Her heart was pounding and her brain was racing.

"I need to know why. How the hell did this happen and how the hell could you do this to me? How the hell you could do this to Kenzie? You owe us that much. You are sleeping with a girl you raised! She was a child John. Is this something that you have been thinking about since before she hit puberty? You disgust me. And yet, yet I still love you. So I need to know. I need to know how we got here."

John looked over at his wife. The woman that he thought he knew. This reaction wasn't what he expected. He expected the tears. He expected her to be on the floor begging him to stop. He could fix it. He was going to leave her, but she never would have gotten half. But infidelity? Well, the judge didn't look to kindly on that.

"She came on to me, Lynne, you have to believe me," John begged as Lynne rolled her eyes. "I never meant for this to happen. When I would come out here for business, I would check on her and make sure she was doing ok. The last little while, well she would open the door and be practically naked, and would walk past me and rub against me, and dammit I am only human! I never meant for this to happen! Please, baby, we can get past this!"

Lynne stared down at the man she loved, and was revolted. She couldn't bring herself to even say anything.

Katherine walked up to her and pulled her arm. "Let's go Lynne."

John kept his eyes on his wife, and she was mesmerized again by his eyes. She was frozen in her tracks.

"You and that dirty slut can go to hell John! Lynne is done with you, and if I have any say in it, you won't have a dime left when she is done!" Katherine shouted pointing in his face.

"Get the hell out of here Katherine, this has nothing to do with you," John said fiercely, eyes shooting daggers at her.

That snapped Lynne back to reality. She looked right at him and punched him in the face and heard bone cracking. She had a lot of rage, and for the first time in her life she felt good about something she had done.

She wasted too many years on him, and as she found out, love was a myth, and you can't focus your whole life on it.

"You bitch!" John started to come at Lynne, but Lynne kept her feet planted. Katherine remembered what Lynne had told her about John's temper, and the times he hit her. Katherine grabbed the first thing she saw and hit him over the head. Lynne's eyes went wide with shock when she saw John's body hit the floor. Katherine had a metal ashtray in her hand, and her chest was heaving. Blood began to leak out on the floor, coming from John's head.

"Oh my god, Kat. Is he dead?" Fear dripped off each word. In an instant, it flashed through her mind that she didn't know if she would be happy or sad if he was dead.

"Lynne, I didn't mean to hit him that hard," Katherine said with her hands still radiating from the vibration of the metal against skull.

Katherine and Lynne stood there, staring, trying to figure out what to do. John didn't move, his body was stiff as the blood poured out on the hard wood floor.

"Check him Katherine," Lynne said calmly as she pushed Katherine towards John's lifeless body. She was still so numb that she felt no emotion.

Katherine knew he was dead, she didn't know much but she knew what a dead body looked like. She witnessed her father dying when he over dosed on drugs. She remembered that feeling, and she knew that John was gone.

"He's gone Lynne, and we have to finish it," Katherine said firmly as she found her composure. She started searching for a piece of paper.

"I need a towel, I don't want to touch anything," Katherine said to Lynne before she walked away.

Lynne walked back to John's lifeless body. After staring for a moment, all her emotions that she held in when she got there came pouring out of her. She had no clue how this escalated, she had no clue what the right way to feel was. She couldn't move. She looked down at him, knowing she would never feel his touch again. She would never see his name come across her phone, and she would never lay next to him in bed. At the same time, she would never have to worry about being hit again, or having to watch what she asks in fear of his temper. John was dead. Lynne was now an accessory to murder.

"Lynne!" Katherine screamed from the kitchen. Lynne snapped out of it and ran back to the kitchen to Katherine. "We still need a towel!" They split up to search for one, and Katherine grabbed the towel off the bathroom floor and went back on her hunt for paper and a pen. Katherine had a big imagination when it came to almost anything, that's how she survived her marriage so long.

Just as Katherine found the paper and pen hidden in a pull-out cabinet in the kitchen, Arielle came in the door.

"What the…" Arielle screamed.

Arielle tried to run back out the door, but Lynne grabbed her. Her instincts kicked right in.

"Get off me!" Arielle shouted as she tried to push away. Katherine ran over and punched her dead in the face, knocking her out cold.

While Arielle was unconscious, they had come up with a plan. Lynne thought Katherine was crazy but she knew this had to be done, and it just might work. Lynne wondered if this day would come back and haunt her, but here and now, her only mission was to finish her revenge, and live free another day.

9.

Arielle slowly came back to consciousness. As her eyes opened, she looked around her home in disbelief. She thought maybe she was dreaming, but she looked down and saw John's body on the floor and realized it was very much real life; her nightmare was just beginning.

"I should kill you, just like I killed him," Katherine said pulling Arielle's head back while she sat tied in the chair.

Lynne walked over to Arielle with hatred and venom in her eyes. She no longer felt that daughterly love.

"How could you do this to me? I treated you like a daughter. I raised you Arielle. I did everything I could for you. I didn't give Kenzie something without giving it to you. I was a mother to you. How could you go and sleep with my husband? A man you called Dad your whole life?"

Lynne's voice rose with each question. She stared into Arielle's eyes, and Arielle felt like she was burning a hole through her soul. She didn't know what to say, she didn't even know how Lynne found out. She was caught off guard and she knew nothing she could say would make things right, or get her out of this. John was supposed to tell her, and Arielle had thought she would just never see or speak to them again. She stared up at Lynne pleading. All she knew is she had one chance to get out of this. Arielle put on a terrified face and looked up at Lynne.

"Speak, or I will kill you!" Katherine shouted.

Katherine was getting angrier with every second that passed. She didn't care Arielle was young enough to be her daughter. All she could think about was how badly this was hurting Lynne. She knew the loss. Finding out the person you love has been unfaithful is a pain most will never understand until they are in it, and Katherine's anger ran deeper than just what he did to Lynne. She was hurt in the same way, and if she had the chance to confront the little slut that wrecked her marriage, she would have. So she had a lot of rage, and was happy to have somewhere to release it.

"Arielle, I am giving you one more chance to explain how you could do this to me," Lynne stated.

"Lynne…mom…Mrs. Walker, I don't know how we got to this point! I swear! It started out he would come visit me and check to see if I was ok. The last little while, well, he brought me presents, took me out and showed me what it was like to be taken care of. After some time, I couldn't help it. He offered to take me out of town, and said he was going to leave you to be with me! He was so handsome, and he broke me. I knew it was wrong! Please, you have to believe me!" Arielle pleaded.

When Arielle finished speaking, Lynne was devastated. She realized that Arielle was not the person she thought she was, and didn't know who to believe. *Doesn't even matter now,* she thought. She was not a daughter to her, and maybe that's what made Lynne the most furious. She put the same love that she had for Kenzie into Arielle, and was betrayed in the worst way.

"You two killed him!" Arielle screamed as she looked around for a way out.

"No, little girl. You killed him," Katherine said as she stood up.

Lynne looked at Katherine, too puzzled to even ask her what she meant by that.

"Here's what is going to happen, Arielle. You are going to write these little love letters to John, telling him how you love him and that if you can't have him, nobody can."

Arielle's eyes went wide as she looked back at Katherine.

"The hell I will," Arielle sputtered.

"You are going to write them, or I'll just kill you and lay you next to him, since you wanted him so badly. You chose," Katherine responded.

Arielle looked to Lynne to save her, begging with her eyes. Lynne barely passed another glance at her.

"What are you going to do?" Arielle said, directing her words at Lynne.

"I'm glad you asked. I am going to teach you a lesson. Clearly, the lessons that Lynne taught you weren't up to your satisfaction, so we will try this again. Trust me, you will have plenty of time to think, and process it. You ruined Lynne and Kenzie's life. The only fair thing is that I ruin yours; An eye for an eye. Start writing!" Katherine demanded.

She shoved Arielle over to the table, and stood over her as she handed her the pen and paper.

After Arielle shakily wrote the letters, Katherine grabbed her arm and dragged her in to the living room and made her place the letters on the table. She took Arielle's hand and placed it over the ashtray that was used to kill John. She smeared his blood on Arielle while Lynne watched, silently. Katherine planned for this to look like a fight gone wrong. It was the perfect cover up. Lynne and Katherine would be gone way before the cops came. All Lynne could think about was Kenzie, and how she would tell her that her father was gone, or that her father had been sleeping with her best friend. She snapped back to the present.

"Kat, are you sure we should do this? I can't go to jail," Lynne said as panic struck her throat as the reality of the situation set in.

"We aren't going to jail."

Katherine's method was more extreme than Lynne could have imagined, but there was nothing that she could do now, unless she wanted to be the one to go to jail.

As she watched Katherine take control of the situation, she thought about some of the little comments over the years that she had made about

John. Katherine knew he wasn't the man Lynne thought he was, she just knew better.

Even though this whole tragedy was a mistake, the look on Kat's face was pure satisfaction, and they were in too deep to back down now.

Katherine went over to Arielle and whispered so quietly that Lynne had to strain her ears to hear. "Everyone has to pay for their mistakes."

She hit her over the head with a lamp to knock her out. She didn't want her dead, just quiet. Arielle needed to be unconscious long enough for her and Lynne to untie her and put everything into place.

When they had the ashtray in place on the floor, they grabbed hands and feet and laid Arielle down on the floor next to John's dead body. Kat went to the kitchen and grabbed a serrated knife from the knife block. She wrapped Arielle's hand around it, and plunged it in to her stomach. *Not deep enough to be a kill stab*, she thought, *but hopefully enough to make it look like she tried to kill herself.*

The two women walked through the house, erasing any sign of themselves. After making sure they wiped any surface they touched, and taking that rag with them they walked back to the crime scene.

Lynne untied Arielle's wrists where she laid on the floor, and wiped a final tear for the daughter she lost.

"When she wakes up, she will realize that she was responsible for John's murder. The police will think it was a crime of passion, and Arielle will take the fall for it. They will see the letters, her prints on the ashtray, and the stab that looks like attempted suicide. It is her fault he's dead, Lynne," Katherine continued quietly. "We have to go now."

No matter what she would say when she woke up, Lynne and Katherine would be long gone and back to their own lives.

In the car, Lynne took a final look at Arielle's house as Katherine pulled out the burner phone that she used for her affairs. She called the local police department about a domestic disturbance at Arielle's house, and that she was worried about the noise. When she hung up Lynne watched in awe as Katherine shattered the phone and launched it out the window. Looking at Lynne, she said, "now it's finished."

Lynne headed back to the airport. She couldn't fathom that she was now a murderer. She was the woman that went after revenge, the one that got her own back, and someone that would remember how this summer would be a new beginning for herself and her daughter, whatever that may be. Still nervous that things wouldn't go as planned, Lynne paced her breathing the whole way back to California. The whole trip had taken a toll on her, and the moment she took focus off her breathing she knew she would break. Every second she was looking over her shoulder and hissing to Katherine that there was no way they were going to get away with this.

She was coming back with her to California in hopes to get the final story worked out. It wasn't like they could talk about it on the plane.

Finally off the flight and back at Lynne's car she had parked at the airport, Katherine turned to Lynne.

"Listen to me, we will never speak on this. We will stick with the story, it's the half-truth. You sensed that he was cheating on you, and you did follow him. Once you found out the truth, you went back home to figure out your life after a divorce. That is why I came back with you, moral support for your planned divorce," Katherine said firmly.

"What about Kenzie?" Lynne asked, still in a daze.

"When it's right, she will know what we want her to know. No problem in hurting her even more," Katherine responded with a shrug. Lynne huffed a sigh and got in the car.

10.

The next morning, Lynne slept late. She was exhausted and was still trying to process everything that happened, and how she was truly feeling. She went down stairs to make some coffee when Kenzie came into the kitchen.

"Hey mom, what's been going on with you?" Kenzie questioned, concerned. She could sense the tension radiating off her mother.

Lynne thought about everything, and didn't want to lie to Kenzie, but she remembered what Katherine said. She did not want to make this worse.

Whatever happened with that tip to the police, she was going to hear about it, so she decided to tell her daughter the half-truth.

"I have something to tell you Kenzie," Lynne said carefully, sitting down at the table in their kitchen.

"Your father has been cheating on me. Kenzie, he has been having an affair with Arielle."

"Mom, what are you talking about?" Kenzie shouted jumping up from the table.

"Kenzie, it's true. That's where I went. I caught them Kenzie. Arielle is not the person you thought she was, hell your father isn't the man I thought I married."

At that moment, Katherine came in and new from the look on Kenzie's face, Lynne told her. She silently went and poured herself a cup of coffee and sat next to Lynne. Kenzie froze in disbelief. Before Kenzie could question her mother more, Lynne pulled out the photos she had taken and held her phone out to her. Kenzie snatched her mother's phone. On the screen staring back at her was her father and Arielle. Her face went sheet white. Lynne walked over to Kenzie and placed her hand on her phone and took it slowly out of her grip and sat Kenzie down.

"Kenzie, I didn't want to believe it either. It hurt me to my core, and I wanted it to be a lie. Your father has shown signs of being unfaithful to me for a long time. There are things in our marriage I've never shared with you. I wanted to protect you, and I didn't want your life to be like mine; filled with stress and worry. I couldn't let that happen to you. I wanted your father and I to have the relationship that you thought we had. I'm so sorry honey."

Kenzie took a deep breath and looked at her mother.

"So what are you going to do mom?"

She stood up grabbing her phone before she could answer.

"What are you doing Kenzie?"

"I'm calling Arielle! I'm calling dad! How could they do this to me? How could they do this to you?" Kenzie started cursing worse than Lynne did when she found out what John had been up to.

"Kenzie, no! Don't call. Promise me you won't, not until you have had a moment to calm down. Promise me."

Kenzie stopped and stared at her mom. She didn't know why her mom would be saying that, but the look she gave her had her putting her phone down. Something bad had happened. Kenzie knew that much.

"Mom, what are you not telling me?" Kenzie said as she looked back and forth between her mother and aunt Kat.

"Kenzie, just do what I'm telling you, please. It's always us honey, remember that."

Lynne lit a cigarette in the house, something she had never done before, and rubbed her temple.

Kenzie saw something different in her mother. She couldn't put her finger on it, but something just wasn't adding up. Where was her dad? Why hadn't he called yet? She didn't understand.

Kenzie walked away from her mom, leaving the kitchen to take in everything her mother just laid on her.

Lynne heard a knock on the door, and went to see who it was. Her stomach dropped considering the recent events. It was the neighbor, delivering a miss delivered package. *Would I always be this jumpy?* She thought. Katherine followed her to the door, and sighed when she saw it was no body. She hugged Lynne tightly and felt her body lag as she sighed with relief.

"Was I wrong to tell her?" Lynne asked quietly, puffing her Marlboro light.

"It was your decision to make, Lynne. The question is, can you live with it," Katherine replied.

"She felt something Katherine, trust me. She knew something wasn't right. I couldn't fully lie to her. I just couldn't. She almost called them but I stopped her and told her to promise not to call."

Just as Katherine began to respond, the doorbell rang again, followed by a bang. They both turned quickly to the door, then back at each other.

Kenzie screamed from the living room. Lynne and Katherine ran into the room to see what was wrong. As they busted in all they heard was the news,

[John walker, 52 years old. A well-known business man's body was found in a Tennessee home. He was brutally beaten. He was pronounced dead at the scene. A young woman was arrested with a stab wound. She is in custody but in critical condition, and her chances of survival are slim. Her name has not yet been released to the public, but it looks as though the two were having an affair. Authorities were notified by an anonymous tip that a domestic disturbance was taking place at the home.]

Kenzie turned to Lynne and Katherine.

"Mom!" Kenzie cried, as she held her hands over her mouth.

The pounding at the door got louder.

"Open up, Police!" an officer shouted from outside their home.

I guess in the end everyone must pay for their mistakes.

Dear Reader,

I really hope you enjoyed this book. I loved living through these characters, and I enjoyed the ride. I hope you did too!

YOUR FEEDBACK MATTERS. Please take a quick moment to write your honest review on AMAZON or barnesandnoble.com. You are so appreciated!

Stay tuned for the next:

Secret life of:

Please visit: www.amirahsbookcollection.com

Subscribe with your email for updates and exclusive blogs on all new books.

Made in the USA
Middletown, DE
19 November 2023